THE CROSSING

For Aspen, with love from Nonna—D. J. N.

For my dad and brothers,
who taught me to love the great outdoors—J. M.

ATHENEUM BOOKS FOR YOUNG READERS
An imprint of Simon & Schuster Children's Publishing Division
1230 Avenue of the Americas, New York, New York 10020
Text copyright © 2011 by Donna Jo Napoli
Illustrations copyright © 2011 by Jim Madsen
All rights reserved, including the right of reproduction in whole or in part in any form.
ATHENEUM BOOKS FOR YOUNG READERS is a registered trademark of Simon & Schuster, Inc.
For information about special discounts for bulk purchases, please contact Simon & Schuster
Special Sales at 1-866-506-1949 or business@simonandschuster.com.
The Simon & Schuster Speakers Bureau can bring authors to your live event.
For more information or to book an event, contact the Simon & Schuster Speakers Bureau at
1-866-248-3049 or visit our website at www.simonspeakers.com.
The text for this book is set in Bulmer MT.
The illustrations for this book are rendered in digital media.
Manufactured in China
0311 SCP
First Edition
2 4 6 8 10 9 7 5 3 1
Library of Congress Cataloging-in-Publication Data
Napoli, Donna Jo, 1948–
The crossing / Donna Jo Napoli ; illustrated by Jim Madsen. — 1st ed.
p. cm.
Summary: In 1805, Sacagawea, a woman of the Shoshoni tribe,
helps Meriwether Lewis and William Clark find a passage to the West Coast,
in this story told through the eyes of the baby boy on Sacagawea's back.
ISBN 978-1-4169-9474-9 (hardcover)
1. Sacagawea—Family—Juvenile fiction.
2. Charbonneau, Jean Baptiste, 1805–1866—Juvenile fiction.
3. Lewis and Clark Expedition (1804–1806)—Juvenile fiction.
[1. Sacagawea—Family—Fiction. 2. Charbonneau, Jean Baptiste, 1805–1866—Fiction.
3. Lewis and Clark Expedition (1804–1806)—Fiction. 4. Shoshoni Indians—Fiction.
5. Indians of North America—Fiction. 6. Overland journeys to the Pacific—Fiction.]
I. Madsen, Jim, 1964– ill. II. Title.
PZ7.N15Cr 2011
[E]—dc22
2010008368

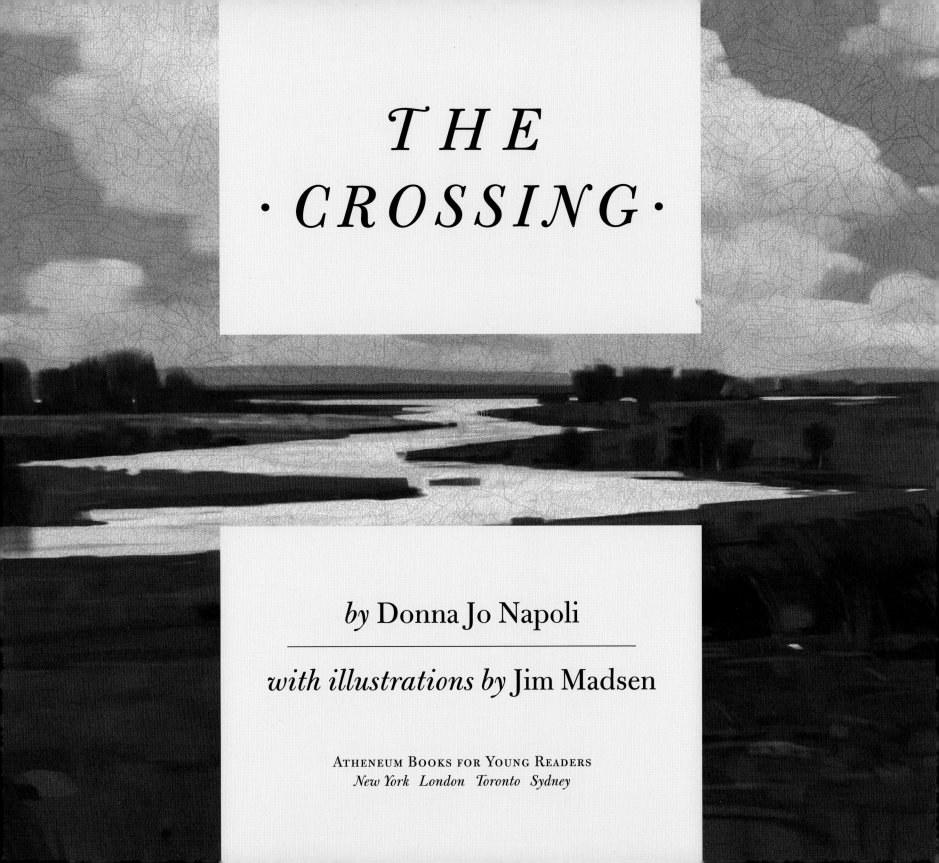

THE · CROSSING ·

by Donna Jo Napoli

with illustrations by Jim Madsen

ATHENEUM BOOKS FOR YOUNG READERS
New York London Toronto Sydney

Rolled in rabbit hide,
I am tucked snug
in a cradle pack
in the whipping cold
of new spring.

Roar, roar!
Grizzlies stand tall in my dreams.

Wind catches the sail,
  swing and woop!
    Over we go, Bia' and Ape' and me—
    Mother and Father and Babe—
splash, shiver.
  Flit, flit,
salmon sparkle
in my dreams.

Red cedars brush the air.
Eagles float
in clouds and blue
of a never-ending, sun-drenched sky,
bleaching the cliffs white.

Scream, hiss!
Cougars prowl in my dreams.

We slip 'round the bend to the waterfall.

No, not one—five! They cascade power in the broiling heat.

Bugle, bugle!

Elks romp in my dreams.

Crude carts
    haul canoes
and supplies
    over broken land
through hailstorms.

We paddle
against the current
till Bia' points
at Beaverhead Rock,
her childhood home at last.

Whoop, whoop,
men dance,
slip, slip,
ermines race
in my dreams.

Up in the Shining Mountains
we find gifts, beads and toys,

and, best of all, a new brother.

Clip, clop,
goats clamber
in my dreams.

Horses twist through mountain passes,
snow everywhere, food so scarce, stomachs so tight.

Kraaa, kraaa!

Nutcrackers call in my dreams.

Out of the mountains
at last,
we enter fierce lands.
But no one is fierce
with me.

Hush, hush,
hands rock me sweet, warm

in my dreams.

Fire
hollows pine
into new canoes
to float
downriver.

Screech, screech!

Owls dive
in my dreams.

We glide
for the first time
with the current
through canyons
that hold rock paintings.

People on shore
hail us down,
smiling.
Children wave.
I grin back.

Thump, thump,
mule deer jump,
yelp, yelp,
dogs shiver
in my dreams.

Dry lands give way
to rain forests.
Storms roll the waters.
We stop for weeks,
and eat roots.

Quek, quek!

Tree frogs serenade
in my dreams.

River again—river, river.
Then, finally, we build
a winter camp on a slope.

The old chief speaks Chinook
to the prisoner, who speaks Shoshoni
to Bia', who speaks Hidatsa
to Ape', who speaks French
to his friend, who speaks English.

Chop, chop, axes cut logs,
Sing, sing, quick tongues make friends
in my dreams.

It rains and rains and rains.
Ape' and Bia' and I
go to the stinking lake—
the Huge Pacific—
and peek through
the bones of a whale.

Squish, squish,
toes dig sand in my dreams.

We try dugouts
     against the mighty spring current.
The current wins.
We buy horses
     and ride.

Buzz, buzz,
I chase bees
in my dreams.

We wait
while snows melt
and spring comes
even to these high mountains.
Then we cross once more.

Snap, snap,

monkeyflowers smell musky
in my dreams.

Summer heat tires us.

Horses get stolen overnight and no one saw a thing.

Clomp, clomp,

I ride horses in my dreams.

Once on the plains
we build dugouts
and ride the river
past rosy boulders.

Leap, leap,

I climb cliffs in my dreams.

One river empties
into another
and carries us home,
where Bia' sets me down
to run and climb and jump for real.

Hurray, hurray!
I run free always and forever
in my dreams.

AUTHOR'S NOTE

On April 7, 1805, Sacagawea, a woman of the Shoshoni tribe, wrapped her baby son, Jean Baptiste, into a cradle board. The baby then began a long journey on his mother's back, with his father at his side. They were helping the pioneers Meriwether Lewis and William Clark find a passage to the west coast.

The journey took them from Fort Mandan, North Dakota, westward into Montana. They traveled in long boats called pirogues. One of the boats flipped over, and important papers fell into the water. They would have been lost, but Sacagawea fished them out.

The summer was hot along the Missouri River. But a bigger problem was the five great falls. The travelers had to portage their boats around them.

They celebrated Independence Day by dancing late into the night. In August they arrived in the Bitterroot Mountains, and visited a Shoshoni tribe. The chief was Sacagawea's brother. They had a wonderful celebration. When they left, the travelers took a small boy with them, to be Jean Baptiste's brother.

That fall they crossed Idaho, traveling on the Clearwater River, then the Snake River, and finally the Columbia River (now known as the Salmon River), past the mudflats of eastern Washington and into the rain forests of western Washington.

As winter set in, they built Fort Clatsop, at a location now known as Astoria, Oregon. Baby Jean Baptiste finally got to run on the beach, free of his cradle pack for a few months.

On the journey, Jean Baptiste saw many wonderful sites—birds flying high, rivers full of fish, and land packed with trees and flowers. He also saw buffalos, cougars, elks, bears, ermines, mule deer, and mountain goats.

By early spring they turned around and headed east again, with Jean Baptiste back in the cradle board. At first they traveled in dugouts. But then they bought horses and rode through the mountains. In the middle of the summer a Crow tribe stole their horses. So they had to make new dugouts.

They paddled east across Montana on the Yellowstone River, until it emptied into the Missouri. Then they retraced their steps home. By mid-August, 1806, they were back where they started.

ACKNOWLEDGMENTS

Thanks to Bill Bright, Ted Fernald, Barry and Robert Furrow, Jim Ronda, and Richard Tchen, who made comments on earlier drafts.

Thanks to Patty Timbimboo-Madsen, the Cultural/Natural Resources Manager of the Northwestern Band of Shoshoni Tribe in Brigham City, Utah, for help on the voice of the story.

Thanks to Bill Reynolds and to the librarians who helped me collect so many reading materials.

Thanks to the many websites I consulted, especially:
www.isu.edu/~loetchri/englishtoshoshoni.htm
www.yourdictionary.com/languages/north.html

And thanks to Brenda Bowen, who suggested I write about the child on Sacagawea's back.

—D. J. N.